DATE DUE

NO 26 '97			
OC 15 '98			
DE 15 '98			
FE 12 '04			
MR 9 '04			

For Jazz

For Jazz 21 SONNETS

Peter McSloy

Linoleum cuts by Nina Mera

hit & run press

Designed by David Bullen

ISBN 0–936156–00–7 (leather)
ISBN 0–936156–01–5 (cloth)
ISBN 0–936156–02–3 (paper)

FIRST EDITION

Published by
hit & run press
P.O. Box 1018
Lafayette CA 94549

To Sue

Contents

Introduction

Jazz music and poetry are two of my most passionate interests. Yet attempts to merge the two usually leave me unmoved. To my mind, they come across as, at worst, crusty relics of a beatnik sensibility or, at best, as merely pale imitations of the free flowing energy of a real jazz performance. Like the albatross in Baudelaire's poem, they flap their wings vainly on the ground, never quite able to achieve the effortless flight of jazz improvisation.

But the jazz sonnets gathered here are another thing entirely. Our poet has penetrated deeply into the jazz art, guiding us to the telling details and epiphinal ecstasies of that world. Most of all, he understands that the apparent free form of jazz is only on the surface, that underneath are unyielding structures, hard as granite. These are the eight and sixteen bar forms — or, even more primal, the twelve bar blues form — that serve to anchor the play of the horns and the flow of the rhythm instruments.

In these poems, the sonnet structure plays a similar role. The rigidity of formalism is made to co-exist with the free play of the words. The result is like a seasoned saxophonist working through the changes of "Body and Soul," telling a story that somehow is comfortably familiar, yet also surprising and new.

Having written about jazz, as well as having played it, I know how difficult it is to capture its essence in words. I have struggled to find the right word, the telling phrase, to describe a recording, a performance, a style, a sound. A beguiling alchemy, to transmute music into language. When I first saw several of these sonnets in a literary journal, I was envious. The fact that they seemed so effortless did not fool me. I knew that in such writing, as in a jazz solo, the phrases that seem the simplest are the ones that often distinguish the masters from the apprentices.

For my own part, when I first ran across them, I immediately wanted to know more about the writer of these exquisite sonnets. Let me share with you some of what I have learned. Peter McSloy, I have discovered, is the pseudonym of Pete Townsend. Some readers may be familiar with the "other" Pete Townshend, a member of the rock group The Who. The only connection between the two, other than a common name and nationality, is that both play the guitar. But while the "other" Townsend excites fans by destroying his instrument on stage, our poet keeps his six string instrument in one piece, using it to play various jazz gigs. When not so engaged, he is active as a writer and university teacher. The name McSloy comes from his mother's family. His grandfather Tom McSloy, a coal miner, was one of the Ashington School of painters in the 1930s and 40s.

The family connection to the visual arts does not surprise me. Reading these poems gives me much of the same enjoyment I experience in looking through books of jazz photos (another of my idle passions). Here is the same pleasure in seizing the beauty of an unexpected moment: tenor saxophonist Ben Webster, who told friends he once knocked down heavyweight champ Joe Louis, uncharacteristically finding time to comb his mother's hair; Clifford Brown stealing down Parisian fire escapes to attend—what, a romantic tête-à-tête?—no, a secret recording session; Charlie Parker, institutionalized in a mental hospital, leaving his horn behind to tend lettuce by the seashore.

Can you capture a life, a career, a sound, an ethos in fourteen lines? Perhaps not. But these sonnets come closer than I would have thought possible before reading them. But then again who would have thought that a twelve bar blues could say so much, continue to say so much, almost a century after it sprouted up in the Mississippi Delta. Let us leave symphonies to the symphonists. I prefer my pleasures in smaller doses. TED GIOIA

For Jazz

Ben Webster

'Frog' for belligerence and a baleful look,
And for the belching tones delivered in a rage
When the tempo rose. He'd buzz and bark
And seem to fight to clear the stage,
And then relax into the broad, warm breeze
He blew, recumbent, couchant on the sound,
Speaking his natural tongue, that priceless ease,
Coaxing a sigh from the hardest reed he found.
Rex Stewart saw him comb his mother's hair
When she was old, and this was Ben
Who cursed, who juiced, who tangled anywhere
With anyone, one of those double-hearted men
Who do not trust the beauty they can make,
And sometimes rip the canvas, for the gesture's sake.

Joe Venuti

An old Italian in an outsize forties suit,
Somebody's Uncle Joe, violin bow in his fist,
Pounding the floor with each determined twist
He gave 'Sweet Georgia Brown'. It was himself, no substitute,
The real Giuseppe, heard half an age before.
'I thought this bloke had died before the war'
Somebody said, no comment needed. Now instead
The amplified attack coursed tirelessly ahead.
During a pause he gave us all a taste
Of 'Trovatore', bellowed in the air,
Unhitched his bow, retied the hair
Over, around the fiddle's narrow waist,
And played that way. Then, taking leave too soon,
'Gen'lmen, ladies, I am out of toon!'

Dexter Gordon

'A country dance was being held in a garden' –
This lyric slowly rumbled in the microphone
To the festival crowd among the olive trees.
Playing the song, the sound would flatten out or harden,
And afterwards he'd elevate the saxophone
Like a sacred host, mocking these ceremonies,
Or maybe burlesquing the whole tired schmeer
Of Europe, and playing jazz, and being here.
Then the giant wakes. The phrases stride
And bite, what seemed uncertainty forgotten.
But this belated turbulence will not subdue
The sense of Dexter standing slightly to one side
While we others try to read an irony begotten
Somewhere between here and Central Avenue.

Lester Young

Everything oblique to Lester: meaning,
Sound, everyone was 'Lady', and he wore
The tenor at an angle, sometimes leaning
Contrariwise in pictures, the model for
The hipsters of the forties. Those early days
He was the greyhound among the bulldogs, he sailed
Out of the section in his hundred darting ways,
Incorrigibly sly, and swift, and veiled.
On clarinet he foretold his fall, a listless
Lack of force not present in his streamlined tenor.
But in the slow decay of sonority and manner,
His final posture was, alone and restless,
Fingering keys he would not allow to speak.
Than which, forever, nothing could be more oblique.

Charlie Parker

Commotions in hotel lobbies, studios,
Arrests and derelictions, leading through
Psychotic wards to the cool Pacific shore.
There he was set to tend the lettuce rows,
To learn to build a wall. At the beach he blew
His alto notes against the breakers' roar,
At night played dances at the hospital,
Innocent, refreshed, congenial.
And in the studio again, the way he ran
Through seven takes in thirty minutes – the ring,
The resonance, the happiness. He posed
With Garner and the others for the camera, the man
At ease, the smiling farmboy, eyes half-closed,
Feeling his strength in that California spring.

Clifford Brown

In some, the qualities come all combined:
Inventiveness both subtle and replete,
With fluent fingers an appraising mind,
A calm controlling the necessary heat
Which is the birthright of the instrument.
No-one had the least hard word to say
In his behalf. They liked his merriment,
His phrasing clean and agile as a cat at play.
In Stockholm, fifty-three, they stole him out
Down fire-escapes, defying Hampton's view
On letting men record in Europe. In France
Their hearing him but once dispelled all doubt
The sessions should be set, as if they knew
To capture him today, while there was still the chance.

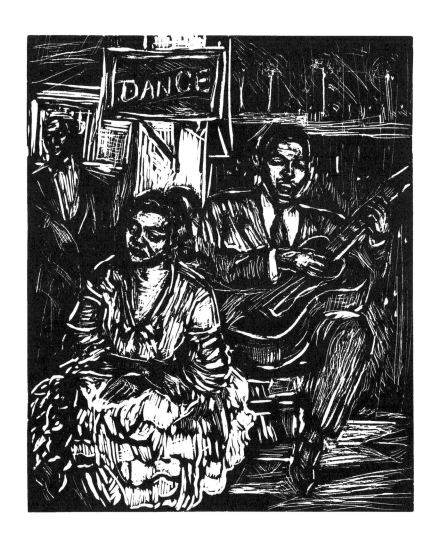

Freddie Green

Time, time. Engine-beat, cat's tread.

Machine that breathes, a bouncing ball, a throb.

Harmonic pulse, knife-edge of walking bass,

Each stroke precisely laid in space,

Moving through slight manipulations of the chord,

For forty years and more, as Schuller said,

A quarter billion beats, he did his job,

He worked his strip of ground, the finger-board.

Rhythm guitar. A craft no-one aspires

To live or die for, too much like lighting fires

In other people's houses. Some of us, though,

By work at small perfections come to know

Great structures rest on every single point.

And the time, the time, was never out of joint.

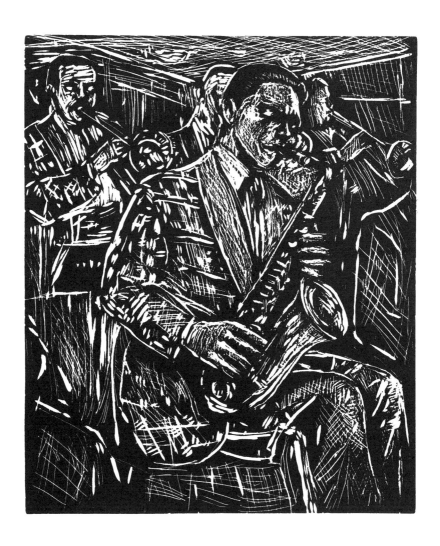

Art Pepper

A damned uncompromising type was Art:
There was the early hard-nosed vanity,
In never running with the Parker pack,
In saturnine good looks, in being smart
The way a hustler has the need to be.
Then, bearing the weight of all this on his back,
Inventing a style that spoke of such a life,
Alert, short-winded, stabbing like a knife.
At last the prison-pale, crop-haired survivor,
With eyes that had seen it all, and still intent
On his choice of ways to drive himself to hell.
The night when he and Stitt allowed no favor,
But each played everything he knew, this meant
Far more than health, than life, this thing he could do well.

Jess Stacy

He owned that kind of lyrical command
That was so much admired. These were the days
Of piano culture in America.
Stacy sat easy, gathered in long-fingered hands
Octaves and basses, and never turned a phrase
That did not evoke some helpless metaphor
Of something crystalline or something clean,
Abstracted but committed, intense and yet serene.
In Goodman's band he was like a hidden spring
In constant flow. Alone, his lines would swing
Lightly, with a deft sustaining tremor. Often enough
It was among the bold brass necks and the tough
Chicago swagger that he placed his clarity:
Silencing a barroom with a line of poetry.

John Coltrane

Polyalphabetic, given to
The multiplying of complexities,
Exhausting every seam, researching through
The most remote of possibilities,
He moved at speed. The sound was brimmed with tension.
There was no resource unable to be used,
No scale or chord whose every permutation
Was not belaboured till the pitches fused.
In nothing but excess was any satisfaction,
The candy bars that wrecked his teeth, each scale
Slonimsky listed practised to destruction.
Until escape was offered in that long folk wail
That broke the bars of theory, in a tone
Not moulded, shaped, but found and used, like stone.

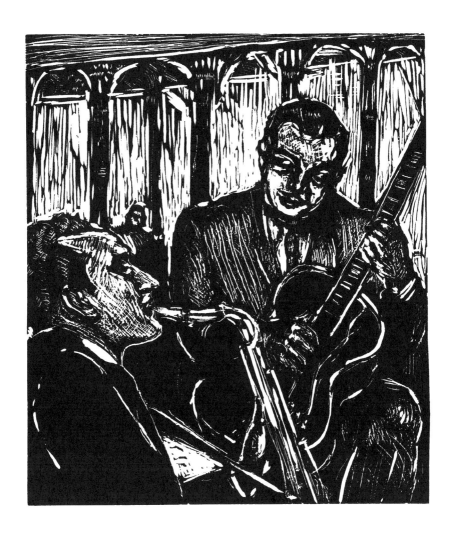

Django Reinhardt

All the records and the music being sold
In Paris, in New York, did not impress
The billiards champion of this little town,
Who fished the river, loitered *chez Fernand,*
And when he played guitar would somehow hold
The strings with crippled fingers. He could care less
They played him on the radio, renown
Means little to a *manouche* artisan.
Booked in Carnegie Hall, he showed up late,
Delayed by some drink or poker game. Such things
Have no importance in the sermons that are read
At Sunday mass at Samois, where there wait
Musician kin at altar side, while there sings
The arc of melody he left in all our heads.

Slim Gaillard

The faces came from Hollywood, Marlene, Judy,
Ava and Clark, affecting A-vout-o-rootie,
To hear Slim serenade sunbathing at Laguna,
Bagels and avocado seeds, or imitate some moony
Cuban balladeer, or radio commercial. In between he
Requested Leo Watson, like some manic scat hyena,
Or shrill Bam Brown to lacerate some tune he
Conjugated with inflections in the King's O-roonie.
He played at times a trenchant swing guitar,
And sparse piano, knuckles-downward style,
The while he'd entertain some slumming movie star
With a mystic, foxy, heavy-lidded smile.
This was the line in which he dealt with fame:
'Hey, Mickey Rooney, what's your second name?'

Art Tatum

Tatum was a world unto himself,
A planet made exempt from gravity,
Where time, though broken, was more orderly,
And moved like some steady continental shelf
Through atmospheres made dense with modulation,
Where speeds could be unearthly, without friction,
But where all loops and swerves through harmony,
However intricate, resolved on certainty.
People say he is too flawless, that he decorates
Compulsively, as though compelled to use
Technique so multitudinous, his heart
Quite disengaged. But listen, how he states
The mighty cadence, in 'Aunt Hagar', of the blues,
Held in the vast precision of his art.

Joe Pass

He said he plays for Joe the barber, recalling
The working Pennsylvania neighbourhoods
And groups of working guys, with evening falling,
Discussing the baseball scores and the price of goods
In Joe or Tony's shop. They want to hear
The good old songs, so one of them will play
Soft rhythm chords, and take the barber's chair,
And furnish a little music to refresh the day.
He walks on stage in London, expecting no
Accompaniment or fanfare, takes his seat
And plays. The songs are now become a flow
Of lines and voices, the style enriched, complete.
But even in this, something still depends
On some hometown parlor where he plays for friends.

Billie Holiday

Billie with her dogs and maid, the years
When she wore down her friends' anxiety,
When the timbre thickened and the voice would give,
Letting audiences indulge a taste for tragedy,
Or sense the presence of authentic tears –
This is the way, in music, women live,
And we applaud the losses they sustain,
And thrill to the female ache in the voice's grain.
Perverse to remember a thing blighted
Better than the same thing whole. Better recall
Billie when her strength could knock men flat,
Drink them under tables, with her fresh, excited
Vigour, laughter, song, in spite of all
Her childhood said. Remember her like that.

Jack Teagarden

He carried in his pocket everywhere
An engineer's peaked cap, for Jack loved trains.
With Kelley's orchestra he roamed the square
From Kansas to the cow-town Texas plains.
Up north they greeted him amazed, he ambled in
To instant acclamation, faced the lights
Of national renown, in those times of bathtub gin,
The radio, the talkies, and the Tunney-Dempsey fights.
Jack was no contender at the public task
Of leading bands. He gave of his solemn cheer
And played and sang his stately blues. We see
In photographs a smiling melancholy mask,
Dreaming of being a quiet engineer
A lazy steady brakeman on the T&P.

Mary Lou Williams

Unseen, she scribbled, by a flashlight, on her knees,
In the back of the bus on those endless all-night drives,
Band scores for Goodman, Ellington. For these
The payments might reach fifty, maybe seventy-five.
The Clouds of Joy ran for a tough decade
On Mary's midnight writings, yet the money
Was always thin, although, she said, they played
Her tunes on every jukebox in the country.
It was on Mary's windowpane that Webster knocked
That night that Hawkins and the Kansas horns were locked
In combat at the Cherry Blossom, Mary who recognised
The art of Monk and Christian, Mary, at sixteen, who surprised
Fats Waller once, matching him note for note. He ran,
Embraced and tossed her in the air, 'laughing like a crazy man'.

Thelonious Monk

There was a stark insistence in his themes.
They ran in circles, beat at a single key,
Plagued dissonances, or otherwise progressed
In simple, steady steps. Everything seemed
Deliberation, circularity.
At the piano he could seem caged, possessed
By the keyboard, one foot pawing at the air,
Bearded and behatted, profoundly unaware.
Nellie ran around him, as you would a child.
But his pathos and his silence were an empty sign
With which the world has never reconciled
That Monk was forever driving through his own design
With a stripped-down logic nothing could deflect,
A school, a strategist, an architect.

Duke Ellington

An epicurean by temperament,
Presenting the look and manner of some benign
But confident seducer, Duke embellished
His mortal time with color more than ornament.
So we imagine he would regally recline
On a cloud of royal purple, from which he relished
The blue of Hodges' alto, the golden-red
Of Williams' trumpet, textures blending in his head.
Or the morning *levée* in some grand hotel,
Duke leisurely transcribing some sensuous impression
That the night has left, while there attend
His pleasure and distraction all the personnel –
Agent, mistress, man of God, physician –
To hide from him that pleasure has an end.

Louis Armstrong

The right acknowledgement of Armstrong's gift
Assumes his iron hold on harmony,
The flawless time dynamic that could lift
The energies of the most phlegmatic company,
The fevered ecstasy of his singing, a personality
Like the sun appearing, and the endless melody
Triumphantly projected, soaring from height to height,
Sound as good money, clear as a cloudless night.
Beyond these things, what we can sometimes miss
Is the streak in him of will, and of decision.
Sweetly irascible, befitting a nature that began
In the Colored Waifs' Home, he was immovable on this:
To play the king, to fill a simple line with passion,
And at the end of it all, to have lived a happy man.

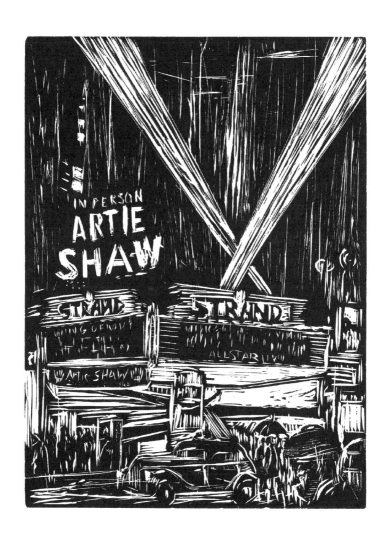

The Bands

"We stood in line outside the Paramount,
  Whole crowds of Jewish and Italian kids
  From Brooklyn. Winter, thirty-eight. The cops
  On horseback. Morning show. We all cut class
  For Berigan with Goodman, or the Count
  With Buck and Lester, to see the trombones fan their lids,
  The trumpet section, standing, blow their tops,
  And four men rhythm, reeds, and eight on brass.
  Jesus, that music made you feel alive!
  Cootie or Vido blasting as the band rose from the pit.
  Mickey Weiss was a fan of Shaw on clarinet
  (Mickey was killed on Guam in forty-five).
  Oh Lord, the Paramount, the Greystone in Detroit,
  The Earle in Philadelphia, Roseland, the Lafayette."

About the Artist

Nina Mera was born in New York in 1947 to Cuban and American parents. Mainly self taught, she began her career as a portrait artist on the Boardwalk in Atlantic City.

She has traveled widely, frequenting the museums of Paris, London, New York and Chicago. Her work has been heavily influenced by the French masters, particularly Toulouse Lautrec.

Along with her pursuit of art, she has studied jazz; performing as a jazz singer, and more recently as a bass player. Her paintings of the contemporary jazz scene and block prints of the jazz greats are flavored by her deep passion for the music.

The illustrations in this book have been hand-printed on 11x15 sheets in a limited edition of 51:

26 boxed sets on Magnani Pescia paper, signed $1,000.

25 individual prints on Daniel Smith Archival paper, signed $100/ea.

To order, contact:

The Jazz Suite

P.O. Box 1404

Ft. Bragg, CA 95437

(707) 964-4038

Colophon

For Jazz was printed in an original edition of 1,000
copies: 100, bound in full leather, numbered and signed
by poet & artist; 200 in cloth; 700 in paperback.

One half of the edition is designated for the USA, the
other half for the UK.